THE AMAZING SPIDER-MAN™

Becoming SPIDER-MAN

BANTAM BOOKS

THE AMAZING SPIDER-MAN: BECOMING SPIDER-MAN
A BANTAM BOOK 978 0 857 51148 5

First published in Great Britain by Bantam Books, an imprint of Random House Children's Books
A Random House Group Company

This edition published 2012

1 3 5 7 9 10 8 6 4 2

Bantam Books are published by Random House Children's Books,
61–63 Uxbridge Road, London W5 5SA

www.kidsatrandomhouse.co.uk   www.totallyrandombooks.co.uk

Addresses for companies within The Random House Group Limited can be found at:
www.randomhouse.co.uk/offices.htm

THE RANDOM HOUSE GROUP Limited Reg. No. 954009

A CIP catalogue record for this book is available from the British Library.

Printed in Italy

This is the story of Peter Parker and how he became the Amazing Spider-Man!

When Peter was a boy, he lived with his parents in a nice house.

Peter would play hide-and-seek in his dad's office. The room was very strange and filled with old things.

One night, someone broke into Peter's dad's office.

This frightened Peter's parents. They had to protect him, so they took Peter to live with Aunt May and Uncle Ben.

Ten years passed, and Peter was all grown up. He was a teenager and went to high school.

Peter enjoyed science and taking pictures.

Peter was just another normal kid. But that was about to change.

One day, Uncle Ben gave
Peter a briefcase that belonged
to Peter's father.

Inside the briefcase was a
picture of Peter's dad standing
with a man named Dr Connors.

Peter decided to find
Dr Connors and ask about
his dad.

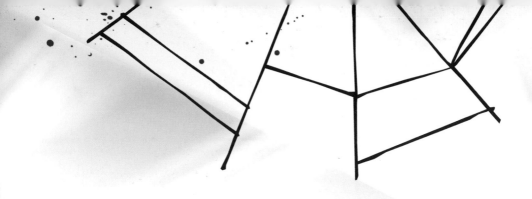

Peter went to a lab called Oscorp where Dr Connors worked.

Peter spoke to Dr Connors, but he wanted to learn more. So he decided to sneak around Oscorp and look for clues.

Peter came to a top secret lab and went inside.

Suddenly, a strange spider came down from the ceiling and bit Peter!

Peter was scared and ran out of the building. But when he got on a train to go home, something strange happened!

The spider bite had given Peter superpowers!

Peter got off the train and
ran all the way home. When he
got there, he was very hungry.

Aunt May and Uncle Ben
watched as Peter ate everything
in the fridge!

Then Peter got very tired and
went to bed.

The next day, Peter learned more about his new superpowers.

He could climb walls. He could run really fast. Peter even had super strength!

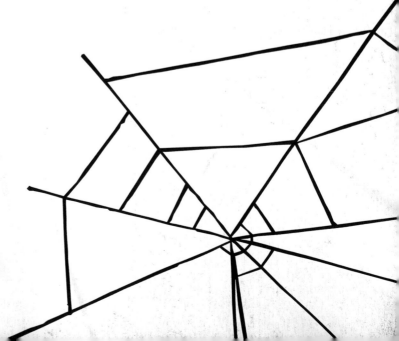

While out practicing with his new powers, Peter fell through a roof and landed in an old gym.

Inside, he saw a huge poster of a wrestler wearing a mask, which gave Peter an idea.

Peter needed to make a costume.

The next day, Peter went to school. He sat at his desk and began to imagine his superhero costume.

Then he started to draw in his notebook. When he looked down, he had drawn his superhero mask!

Peter's costume was almost done!

Peter raced home and went to his room.

He began to work on his costume, using red and blue cloth.

He sewed and sewed.

After a few hours, Peter was done!

It fit perfectly! But something was still missing.

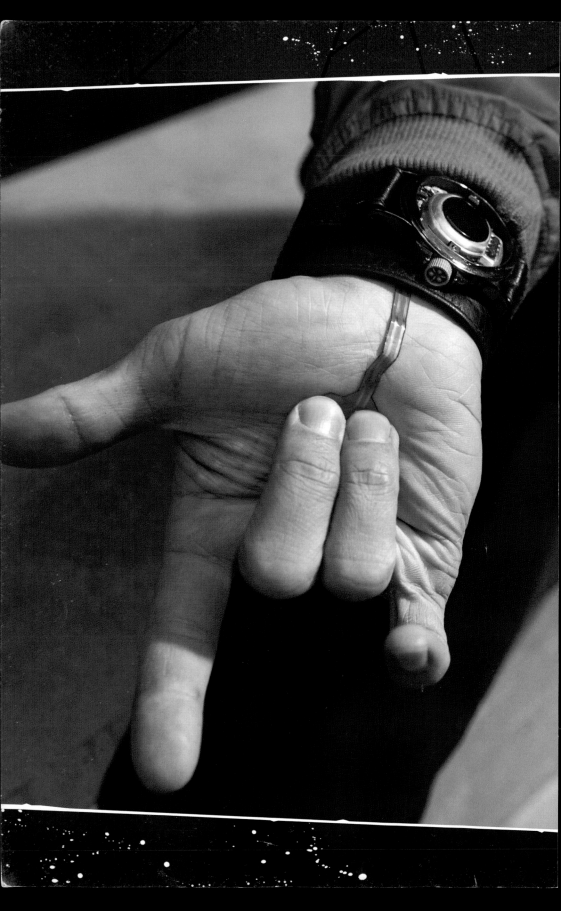

Peter needed something that would help him swing from building to building.

At Oscorp he found a special web fluid. It was very strong and very sticky.

Peter went home and made a web-shooter device.

Now he could spin a web – just like a spider!

Peter went out and tested his new costume and web-shooters.

Peter swung through New York City. He was a natural! He even stopped a car thief!

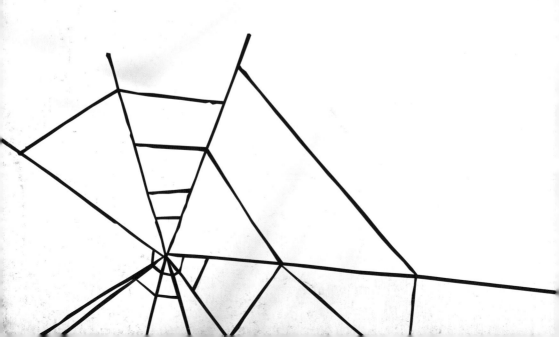

All Peter needed was a cool superhero name to go along with his costume.

And so he chose the Amazing Spider-Man!

Peter Parker had come a long way from being a kid in high school.

He was now a superhero with great powers . . . and a great responsibility to help others.

And Peter would do it as the Amazing Spider-Man!